STRANGE NEIGHBORS

STRANGE NEIGHBORS

MARY LABATT

KIDS CAN PRESS

Kids Can Press acknowledges the financial support of the Ontario Arts Council,
the Canada Council for the Arts and the Government of Canada, through the
BPIDP, for our publishing activity.

Published in Canada by
Kids Can Press Ltd.
29 Birch Avenue
Toronto, ON M4V 1E2

Published in the U.S. by
Kids Can Press Ltd.
2250 Military Road
Tonawanda, NY 14150

www.kidscanpress.com

Edited by Charis Wahl
Designed by Marie Bartholomew
Typeset by Karen Birkemoe
Printed and bound in Canada

CM   00 0 9 8 7 6 5 4 3 2
CM PA 00 0 9 8 7 6 5 4 3 2 1

Canadian Cataloguing in Publication Data
Labatt, Mary, date
    Strange neighbors

(Sam, dog detective)
ISBN 1-55074-603-0 (bound)   ISBN 1-55074-605-7 (pbk.)

I. Title. II. Series: Labatt, Mary, date. Sam, dog detective.

PS8573.A135S77 2000   jC813'.54   C99-932554-X
PZ7.L32St 2000

Kids Can Press is a Nelvana company

To my daughter, Elizabeth,
Who is an animal lover,
With my love

1. What Sam Saw

All morning Sam sprawled on the sofa while the clock ticked loudly in the empty house. From outside, she heard brakes screech and doors slam.

Sleepily, she looked over the back of the sofa. *A moving van. Big deal,* she thought. *Who cares if somebody moves in next door to Jennie?* She slumped back down. *I'm starving and I'm bored.*

Sam closed her eyes and dreamed of a cheesy, gooey pizza covered in ketchup. Just as she was thinking about her first bite, there was a loud bang.

Sam poked her head through the lace curtain so she could see better. The movers had dropped a wooden crate.

"Don't touch!" yelled the tall, thin man backing away from the box.

"Yikes!" shouted the short, fat man.

Then Sam saw it. Out of the box's broken corner came a small animal. Then another ... and another ... and another ... On and on they came out of the crate. They hopped across Jennie's lawn and across Sam's yard.

Toads! Ugly, warty toads! In amazement, Sam watched the long line of toads disappear down the street toward the field.

"I've never seen anything like that," muttered the fat man.

"Don't drop another box," warned the tall one. "It could have snakes in it!"

Sam watched the movers pick up the next box very carefully.

What would the new neighbors want with toads? Sam asked herself. *They'd make disgusting pets.*

For the rest of the day Sam thought about the toads while she waited for Jennie to come after school. Sam's owners worked all day, so they hired the little girl next door to take Sam for walks.

At last a key turned in the front door.

Sam hopped off the sofa and slurped at Jennie's face. *About time! Joan and Bob don't care how lonely I get.*

Ten-year-old Jennie Levinsky hugged the big sheepdog tightly. "I love dog-sitting you, Sam," she giggled, as she wiped her face and her long brown hair with her sleeve.

Sam stopped slurping. *I'm bored and I'm starving.* She stared at Jennie. *But something interesting happened today.*

Jennie could hear what Sam was thinking. The first day Sam talked to her, they were having a picnic. Suddenly Jennie heard someone say that they wouldn't drink creek water. Jennie had looked everywhere for the voice. Finally, she realized it was Sam.

Sam had just stared at her, and Jennie heard, *I knew you'd be able to hear me. Most dogs are too stupid to notice when someone has the gift. Very few people have it, and I can always tell.*

From then on, Sam talked to Jennie all the time. Nobody knew except Jennie's best friend, Beth Morrison. It was Jennie's secret.

Jennie looked lovingly at Sam's furry face and round black nose. "What was so interesting today?"

Toads. The new neighbors have toads.

"Toads? How do you know?"

I saw them.

"How? You've been inside all day."

It was the movers' fault.

Jennie's brown eyes twinkled. "Sam, you're a terrible storyteller."

Sam sniffed. *I am a great storyteller. The movers dropped the box. That's what I've been telling you.*

At last Jennie understood. "Oh. The movers dropped a box and toads came out?"

Sam glared at Jennie. *That's what I said.*

"Nobody wants toads." Jennie looked puzzled.

The neighbors do. The toads hopped across our yards and went into the field. Sam thought for a moment. *They must have been trained toads. They hopped in a line.*

Jennie wrinkled her nose. "Who would want trained toads?"

People who own a circus.

"I never saw toads in a circus."

Maybe they jump through hoops.

Jennie laughed. "You're crazy, Sam! Nobody would go to a circus to see toads!"

Sam sniffed. *No need to be insulting. All I know is that they were trained toads. And they were going to live next door to you, until the movers dropped the box.*

Jennie patted Sam's big head gently. "I didn't mean to insult you." Her face brightened. "I bet you're hungry."

Yes! I want pumpkin pie with nachos.

Jennie stopped at the kitchen door. "Joan told me to feed you dog food."

Nobody is ever going to make me eat Liver Delight. Sam climbed back up on the sofa.

And that's final.

2. Something's Strange

At dinner, Jennie's family talked about the new neighbors.

"They rented that house in a big hurry," said Mrs. Levinsky, as she dished out mashed potatoes.

"They didn't even look at it!" exclaimed Jennie's dad, spooning peas onto his plate.

"That's strange," murmured her mother. "Nobody rents a house without looking at it."

"They must be weird." Jennie cut her sausages into little pieces. "Sam says they brought toads."

Her thirteen-year-old brother's spiky blond head whipped up. "Sam says," Noel mimicked.

"Do you still talk to that big lump of fur?"

Jennie's heart sank. She would never hear the end of this. "Uh– Uh– I didn't mean that."

Noel squinted suspiciously. "What else did Sam say?" Potatoes bubbled out of his mouth.

Jennie's face grew hot. "S-Sam didn't say there were toads. I just know there were toads."

Their father leaned forward. "What's this about toads?"

Jennie took a deep breath. "The movers dropped a box and a bunch of toads hopped out. They must be trained because they hopped down the street in a straight line."

"Why would anybody want toads?" Jennie's mother stopped eating.

Jennie's father looked puzzled. "And why would anybody train them to walk in a line?"

After their walk that night, Sam jumped on Jennie's bed. *I need some excitement! I'm a great*

detective and I want a new case.

Jennie ripped open a bag of cheese puffs and started to nibble.

Sam's head whipped up. *Hey! What about me!*

Jennie was about to say that Sam shouldn't eat people food, but it was no use. She scattered a few cheese puffs on her bed.

Sam lapped them up lazily. *I think there's something very weird about the new neighbors. Maybe that'll be the case I'm looking for.*

"Let's leave the new neighbors alone." Jennie tossed Sam some more cheese puffs. "I don't want to get in trouble."

Detectives don't care about trouble. Sam munched noisily. *Tomorrow is Saturday. Joan said that's when the new neighbors arrive.*

Sam looked out the window. *We can see perfectly from your bed, Jennie.* She spewed crumbs as she crunched. *I'll come over in the morning so we can watch. There's a mystery about those toads.*

I just know it.

3. The New Neighbors

I TOLD YOU THEY WERE WEIRD.

Early Saturday morning, Sam scratched at Jennie's back door. Jennie's mom opened the door and smiled.

Sam wiggled as Mrs. Levinsky patted her big head. "Good girl."

Sam stopped wiggling. *Who cares about being a good girl?* She marched up the stairs to Jennie's room. *I'll tell you what I care about. I care about being a great detective.*

Rumpled and sleepy, Jennie yawned and opened her eyes.

Hurry up. The toad people are coming today. Sam jumped on the crumpled sheets, leaving a trail of muddy paw prints.

"Sam!" yelled Jennie. "We'll get in trouble for that."

Sam wasn't worried. *Phooey. Your mother thinks I'm too stupid to know about footprints. She pats me on the head and says "good girl" like I'm an idiot.*

Sam looked around. *Where's breakfast?*

In a few minutes, Jennie was back with a large box of sugar-coated cereal.

I love that stuff!

Sam was gobbling the last piece when they heard a car. *They're here!* While Sam pressed her nose against the window, Jennie peered over her shoulder.

On the street below, a strange car screeched to a stop. Bright pink paint, fins and chrome strips made the car look as if it had been driven out of an old movie. Three doors flew open and three women spilled out. They were as odd-looking as their car.

The driver was short and dumpy with a wild mane of orange hair. She folded an enormous orange plaid cloak across her round little body. Legs like sausages poked out of the cloak.

Hello there, Pumpkin. We're your new neighbors.

Jennie giggled.

The second one was tall and thin with cat's-eye glasses and smooth black hair. Everything about her was pointy – her nose, her chin, her shoes, her fingers.

Spider Lady. That's what I'm naming that one.

"I'm glad they can't hear you." Jennie hugged Sam and laughed.

The third woman had blond hair piled up like candy floss. Her skirt was short and her heels were so high that she wobbled when she walked.

I'm calling her High Heels. Those are the stupidest shoes I've ever seen.

An angry yowl came from the car and Spider Lady leaned over to open the other door. "Sorry, baby," she rasped. "Mama didn't mean to ignore you."

Like a stately king, a mangy black cat emerged from the car. One eye was closed, one ear was torn, and his fur stood up in matted spikes. He sat on the sidewalk and meowed furiously.

"Mama said she was sorry," squawked Spider Lady.

"Baby!" gushed Pumpkin.

The cat turned slowly and eyed her with hatred.

"Mama loves her little baby." Pumpkin clasped her pudgy hands happily.

I don't believe this. Sam rolled her eyes.

High Heels tottered toward the cat. "Come to mama, darling," she crooned. "Mama has cat treats."

The cat stared at her with disgust.

How many mamas does that ugly thing have?

At that moment the three women turned to their new house and smiled.

"Lovely, isn't it?" Pumpkin crooned.

"Beautiful!" croaked Spider Lady.

"Perfect!" murmured High Heels. "We'd

better see if everything's all right."

Sam chuckled. *They're looking for their toads.*

The three women hurried toward their house. Behind them, the battle-scarred cat followed slowly.

"How is everybody?" Pumpkin called, as they opened the front door.

Everybody's in the woods. Sam snickered.

Suddenly there was shriek. "Oh no!"

4. Who Wants Toads?

"You're lucky to have strange neighbors!" cried Beth. As she swung on her porch swing, sunlight danced on her fluffy red hair. "There's nobody weird on my street!"

Just then, Beth's twin brothers piled out the door. "Sam!" they screamed.

I love five-year-olds. I bet I get snacks out of these guys. With a happy woof, Sam jumped off the porch.

Within minutes, Sam was back covered in strawberry ice cream. Licking her chops, she blinked calmly at Jennie. *Don't start the dog food speech.*

Jennie scowled.

Beth was still thinking about Jennie's new neighbors. "Why would they want toads?"

"Want to know something really weird?" Jennie leaned toward Beth.

"What?"

"The toads hopped in a line. They must be trained."

"Nobody trains toads!" exclaimed Beth.

Jennie shrugged. "I know. It doesn't make sense."

"What would they use toads for?" Beth chewed on a fingernail as she swung back and forth.

"Sam thinks they're in a circus."

Beth screwed up her small face. "That's the stupidest thing I've ever heard!"

Sam squinted coldly at the girls. *Tell Beth to watch who she calls stupid.*

Jennie rubbed Sam's ears. "Nobody would buy a ticket to see a bunch of toads, Sam," she whispered.

Hmph.

"Let's think," said Beth. "Who uses toads?"

"Maybe they eat them." Jennie twisted her long hair into a ponytail.

Sam's head whipped up. *Never! Toads are the worst-tasting things in the world. I bit one once. Aggh! Worse than Liver Delight!*

"Sam says toads taste terrible."

"Maybe they're using them in science experiments."

Hmm, mad scientists ... I bet an experiment went wrong ... I bet those toads used to be people ... That's why they can hop in a line ... They got turned into toads and they're in the woods right now crying about it.

"Those women didn't look like scientists, Sam," objected Jennie.

Sam's mind was whirring. *Then it must be a magic spell ... Maybe the toads are waiting for a princess to kiss them ...*

"Sam thinks it might be magic."

Beth stopped swinging. "Magic?"

Yeah. Magic. Tell her, Jennie ... Trolls grabbing kids to turn them into toads ... Princes getting turned into toads by a witch ... Stuff like that.

"Sam's talking about magic and trolls and witches and stuff," said Jennie.

Beth's green eyes sparkled. "Witches use toads," she said. "Witches use them in their potions!"

"Witches?" echoed Jennie.

"Witches," repeated Beth. "I don't know anybody else who wants toads. Only witches."

The hair over Sam's eyes lifted with interest. *Hmm. Witches would be good.* She stared at Jennie. *A few witches next door would be lovely.*

Jennie frowned.

So, let's spy on them.

"We could get caught!" protested Jennie.

Phooey. Danger is part of detective work.

Sam started to pace. *I'm going to find out why those weird people brought toads to Woodford. I bet they are witches.* She stopped and stared at Jennie. *I wonder who they came to put a spell on.*

"They didn't come to put a spell on anybody, Sam," said Jennie. "They're not witches."

Beth heaved a huge sigh. "It makes me crazy when you and Sam talk. I wish I could hear her."

"So do I." Jennie slumped down in a porch chair. "Then you could argue with her."

"But maybe they really are witches, Jennie." Beth stroked Sam's head. "Who else would have toads?"

Yeah. Why did they come to Woodford? Sam stared hard at Jennie. *Maybe they came to put a spell on you.*

"They wouldn't come for me, Sam," sighed Jennie. "I haven't done anything to anybody."

"You don't have to do anything," said Beth. "Witches just pick someone. Sometimes," she added darkly, "they put a hex on the whole town."

Wow! thought Sam happily. *The whole town under a spell!* Sam nudged Jennie with her nose. *Don't you think it's odd that they rented the house so fast?*

"It is odd," Jennie admitted.

"What's odd?" asked Beth.

"The neighbors didn't even look at the house before they rented it."

"That's not normal." Beth leaned forward

eagerly. "My parents looked at our house ten times."

They don't care about the house! They just need a place to cast their spells. Sam danced happily across the porch. *Witches are great! Hags with warts and long fingernails . . . Witches with long noses and hairs on their chin . . . Witches with spooky black cats.* Sam stopped and whirled around. *They've got a black cat, Jennie! They're witches for sure!*

"Maybe they are," grumbled Jennie. "But we should leave them alone."

"Don't worry, Jennie," said Beth cheerfully. "Sam will protect us."

Never forget my fabulous teeth! Witches can't taste worse than toads.

Jennie sighed.

Little tingles of excitement prickled up and down Sam's spine. *Life is looking up. Now . . . where's the food?*

When Jennie and Sam came back from Beth's house, the new neighbors were sitting on Jennie's sofa!

A growl rumbled deep in Sam's throat. Jennie's mouth fell open.

Spider Lady folded her long, skinny arms and legs. "What a fine little girl."

"Hello," oozed High Heels. "Nice to meet you."

"What a charming child," trilled Pumpkin, smacking her fat lips.

"Lovely," they all cooed. "Lovely."

Jennie's mom bustled in with coffee. "Sit down, Jennie, and meet the new neighbors." Mrs. Levinsky introduced them, but Jennie was too shocked to catch their names.

Mrs. Levinsky smiled. "They're sisters, Jennie. Isn't it nice to have new neighbors?"

"What a perfect little girl," murmured the sisters, licking their lips.

Jennie felt as if she was pinned to her chair.

5. Somebody's Watching Us!

For the next few days after school, Sam and Jennie spied on the neighbors through a crack in Jennie's back fence. But all they ever saw was the cat sunning himself on the steps.

I hate cats, said Sam. *Almost as much as I hate teenagers.*

Jennie giggled. "He sure is ugly, isn't he?"

Just then, Pumpkin poked her fluffy orange head out the door. "Such a cute baby," she gushed at the cat.

The cat hissed in her face.

Pumpkin smiled happily. "You are mama's little baby."

Crazy Mama needs a new baby.

A nearby squawk made Sam and Jennie jump. Looking up, they saw a crow sitting on the fencepost. Its black feathers ruffled in the breeze.

"Caw! Caw!" the crow shrieked, its bright, beady eyes boring into them.

"H-h-h-hello," stammered Jennie.

Nobody says hello to birds.

"What should we say then? It's staring at us."

Let it stare. "Woof!"

The bird threw back its shiny head and cackled.

A chill crawled through Jennie. "That's a creepy bird," she whispered.

Who cares? "Woof!"

The crow leaned over the fence and squawked at them again. Like a tiny snake, its pointy tongue darted in and out.

"Caw!" it screeched and flew away.

Beth and Jennie decided to go to the library and get a book about witches.

Sam eyed the book with distaste. *I hate reading. Just look for the facts.*

Jennie giggled. "Sam just wants the facts."

Beth sat down on the back steps and opened the book. "It says witches can ride through the air on a broomstick."

Everyone knows that.

Jennie peered over Beth's shoulder and pointed. "Look, Beth. It says witches can be men or women."

Find something we don't know.

Beth leaned over the book. "Hey! Look at this! Witches can change the weather!"

Jennie read the next page and gasped. "It says they can take the form of animals, too! Maybe the crow was a witch!"

Now that's interesting ...

"Look." Beth jabbed her finger at another page. "A group of witches is called a coven."

Big deal.

"They meet four times a year to make plans."

Hmm ... Sam pictured a smoky cave filled with black-cloaked witches. At the front, surrounded by candles, the head witch read out plans to the chanting coven. When he looked up, his red eyes shone with evil.

Jennie was watching Sam. "Don't think up anything too scary, Sam."

Phooey. I'm never scared.

Beth ran her finger down the page as she read. "Witches use a book of recipes to mix their potions ... They mix them in a black pot called a cauldron ... They put horrible things in their potions – like lizards, toads or worms."

Toads, huh?

Beth stopped reading and closed the book. "It says a witch's book is rarely found."

Sam's mind whirred. *Perfect! Let's find out how they brew their spells. Let's watch to see if they fly around on broomsticks. Let's –*

"Sam," interrupted Jennie firmly, "I think we should stay away from them."

Sam gave Jennie a pleading look. *Come on, Jennie. I need some excitement. I'm a famous detective and I have nothing to detect.*

Jennie opened her mouth to reply when a shadow fell across the porch. They looked up to see the crow perched on a flower basket.

"Caw!" it shrieked. "Caw! Caw! Caw!"

The bird stared at them until they squirmed. Then it squawked horribly and flew away.

6. They're up to Something!

Late that afternoon a towering storm gathered over Woodford. Black scudding clouds raced through the sky. Whistling winds peeled the shingles off roofs.

Jennie, Beth and Sam huddled in Jennie's room. Sheets of rain poured down the windows, and the thunder was deafening.

Wow! Sam crawled under the bed. *This is a big one.*

At last, the storm was over. The air outside smelled fresh, but there was litter everywhere.

"Every flower in my garden is smashed!" Jennie's mother wailed.

As soon as she got home, Beth phoned to say

that all the gardens on her street were flattened, too. Her mother was really upset.

When Jennie's dad came home he had more news. On the car radio it said the crops around Woodford had been destroyed. Four cows had been killed by lightning, and a dog had been electrocuted. "What an awful storm," he kept muttering. "We've never had anything like this before."

Pictures of devastation greeted them on the TV screen. Barns were blown down. Hay was squashed flat. "The worst storm to hit the area since 1891," the announcer said.

That night the phone rang at nine o'clock. Jennie heard her mom saying, "Well, it is a little late, Beth. Jennie's in bed … All right … just for five minutes."

"Jennie," Beth breathed into the phone. "Make sure nobody is listening."

Jennie looked around. "It's okay."

"Jennie, this is serious. I'm reading another book on witches." Beth paused. "One of the first signs that witches are casting spells is weird weather."

"Weather?" Jennie blinked.

"Casting a spell causes a huge weather disturbance." Beth took a deep breath. "Jennie, the radio says there's going to be another storm tomorrow."

"Oh no!" gasped Jennie.

"They're up to something." Beth's voice was grim. "And you're right next door!"

The next storm was worse. When the first flat rain drops spat on the ground, Jennie and Beth decided to get Sam.

Jennie's older brother Noel laughed as they dashed out the back door. "Is the poor little doggie scared?"

Jennie and Beth didn't stop to answer.

When Jennie and Beth burst back in the door with Sam, the rain was pelting down. They stood dripping in the kitchen.

Noel was making an after-school snack. "So this walking fur coat is a big chicken, huh?"

Sam tried to shake water on him. *Tell him to shut up.*

"Shut up, Noel," said Jennie.

Noel chomped on his sandwich. "What a sissy this dog is." Sandwich bits hung from his braces.

Sam glowered at him. *I can't tell you how much I hate teenagers.*

"Ignore him." Jennie led her friends up the stairs. "It's the only way."

Snug in Jennie's room, the girls closed the curtains and tried to shut out the storm. But every time the thunder crashed, they held their breath.

So where's the food? Stress makes me hungry.

"Be right back." In no time Jennie reappeared with a giant bag of vanilla cookies.

Yum. You wouldn't have a little ketchup for these, would you?

"Forget it, Sam."

Hmph. Just thought I'd ask.

As they were crunching cookies, they became aware of a different sound. The wind had slowed, and there was a strange drumming above their heads.

What's happening? Sam hopped up on the bed and poked her head under the curtains to look out. Hailstones the size of golf balls bounced crazily on the street and lawns.

The three friends watched the world turn white before their eyes. In minutes it was winter – an eerie winter with lightning flashing over whiteness.

Sam was jubilant. *It's the witches!* She pranced around the bed. *I can't wait to find out what they're doing!*

"Those witches must be casting a spell," whispered Beth.

"Maybe they're putting a hex on the town." Jennie's voice sounded hollow.

Maybe they'll turn us all into toads! Sam's feet whipped the quilt into little mounds as she danced.

Jennie whirled to face Sam. "I don't want to be a toad, Sam! I like being a person!"

"I hope that's not what they're doing," Beth said in a small voice. "I would hate to be a toad."

7. Jennie's Terrible News

RELAX. I'LL THINK OF SOMETHING.

On Saturday, Jennie got the shock of her life. She went to get Sam.

What's the matter? You're white as a ghost.

Without answering, Jennie rushed Sam out the door and headed toward Beth's house.

Sam ran beside her. *So tell me.*

"I can't tell you now." Jennie jerked her head at the houses. "Look!"

The three sisters were waving happily from their front window.

"I bet witches can hear through walls," Jennie whispered.

Hmm ... Maybe they can.

Through the peaceful Woodford streets,

Jennie and Sam ran to Beth's house. Jennie thought she could hear the witches cackling behind her.

"Hello, Jennie." Mrs. Morrison smiled when she opened the front door. "Hi, Sam."

Behind her, two red heads poked out. Sam barked, and David and Daniel squealed. "Sam's saying hello!" they yelled.

Jennie didn't want to waste time. "May we go to Beth's room?" She tried to sound polite.

Just then, Beth appeared on the stairs. "Come on up, Jennie. I've got some new books to show you."

Sam bounded up the stairs with the girls. Jennie shut Beth's door behind them.

"Something terrible has happened!" Jennie leaned on the door. "I've never been in this much trouble in my life!"

Beth looked worried. "What happened?"

"You're not going to believe it."

So tell us.

Jennie's face was chalk white and her voice was tiny. "The w-witches are b-baby-sitting me every day after school."

"What!" screamed Beth.

What!

"My mom has to stay late at our drugstore because it's really busy. She's sending me to the witches!"

Beth was thunderstruck. "I don't believe it."

Sam sat down with a thud. *I don't either.*

"It's true!"

"Why can't you stay with Noel?"

"Because he has football practice every day this month." Jennie chewed her lip anxiously.

"Noel should quit football," said Beth. "Staying with witches is dangerous."

"I know," said Jennie.

"Tell your parents you hate the neighbors."

"I did."

"Tell them you think they're creepy."

"I did."

"Tell them they're witches."

"I did."

"Tell them you're not going."

"I did."

Jennie slid down the door and slumped to the floor. "Nothing worked. I have to go on Monday." Jennie put her head in her hands. "My parents won't listen. They keep saying how nice the new neighbors are."

Sam licked Jennie's hands. *Don't worry, kid.*

Jennie raised a tearstained face. "What am I going to do?"

Relax. I'll think of something.

8. Friends Stick Together

JENNIE'S LUCKY SHE'S GOT ME.

The next day Sam and Beth had more ideas.

Forget the witches. We can run away together. We'll live in the woods.

"Say you want to go and live with your grandmother," offered Beth.

Ask Beth's mother to baby-sit.

For a split second, Jennie brightened. "Could I come to your house, Beth?"

Sadly, Beth shook her head. "I already asked my mother. She's taking the twins to swimming lessons. I have to go with them."

Jennie stared hopelessly at the ceiling.

"Hah! I've got it!" Beth kicked the bed. "I'm going to the witches with you, Jennie."

Jennie sat up. "You are?"

"Yeah." Beth stuck out her jaw. "I don't want to watch the twins swim. My mom will let me go with you."

I'll come, too. Then you'll be safe.

Jennie felt a glimmer of hope. "Sam says she's coming, too."

Sam lifted her head proudly. *Those witches better watch out. My teeth are wonderful.*

Beth turned to Jennie. "Don't worry. We'll be there."

After all, what are friends for?

On Monday after school, the three friends knocked at the witches' door. When the door opened, three faces leered at them.

"You've brought your little friends," gushed Pumpkin.

"Friends," rasped Spider Lady as she laced her long sharp fingers together. "I love friends."

"The more the merrier, I always say." High Heels tottered into the hall.

"Yeeeeeoow!" shrieked the cat and spat in Sam's face.

"Woof!" said Sam.

"Sssss," hissed the cat.

Oh, go away.

Pumpkin picked up the scruffy cat and rocked him back and forth. He squinted at her with one wicked eye.

"Mama's little baby," she sang softly into his chewed ear.

The cat looked down at Sam and drew his lips back from his sharp little teeth. "Ssssss."

Shut up. You're ugly and you stink.

"This is Rupert." Spider Lady pointed a long bony finger at the cat. "He's our baby."

Rupert hissed again, leaped out of Pumpkin's arms, and disappeared.

"He's shy," Spider Lady explained.

Anybody that ugly should be shy.

"Come in," Pumpkin oozed in a hungry voice.

High Heels licked her red lips. "Follow me."

Spider Lady grinned as if she expected a feast. Her pointy little teeth were just like the cat's.

When Jennie, Beth and Sam stepped into the living room, they gasped.

Giggling, the witches loomed over them. "Do you like it?"

The living room was painted bright red. Caged lizards, snakes, hamsters and rats were stacked in every corner. In one cage sat a blotchy guinea pig. From somewhere in the house came a sad whining sound.

"You sure have a lot of pets," blurted Beth.

"We do indeed." Pumpkin's plump jowls folded into a smile. "We love animals."

"Come and see our baby." High Heels teetered toward a door at the end of the room.

I thought that ugly cat was the baby.

The door opened to a sunroom. There in a cage was the worst-looking parrot Sam had ever seen. Broken feathers stuck out all over its body. It glared at them horribly.

"Y-you collect animals," stammered Jennie.

The sisters cackled loudly. "You might say that."

"Sit down," urged Pumpkin. "Tell us who your friends are, Jennie."

Jennie, Beth and Sam perched on the edge of the sunroom sofa under the parrot's angry gaze.

"You've met Sam. I dog-sit her when her owners are at work." Jennie gulped. "And this is Beth."

Beth smiled politely at the witches.

"You're a pretty little girl," crooned Pumpkin. "Isn't she, sisters?"

"Very pretty," they agreed.

Jennie and Beth shifted uncomfortably on the sofa.

Sam eyed the three women suspiciously. *Do witches eat kids?*

Spider Lady leaned forward in her chair. "Why did you bring your friends with you, Jennie?"

Because we know you're witches. Jennie's friends are here to protect her.

Jennie squirmed. "B-B-B-Beth has no one to baby-sit her, so I said she could come." Spider Lady's slitty eyes bored into her. "And Sam gets lonely."

Three heads turned to stare at Sam. "That's quite all right." Three pairs of loving eyes caressed her. "Quite all right."

Sam shivered. *Maybe they eat dogs!*

9. What's for Dinner?

Every day after school, the three friends went to the neighbors' house. Every day they were welcomed as though they were long-lost cousins. Every day they sat stiffly in the living room eyeing the little animals, wondering if they used to be people.

In the kitchen, a huge black pot was always boiling on the stove. As she stirred, Pumpkin emptied little bottles into the brew. Then she put the bottles high up in a cupboard.

Sam watched carefully. *Look at that! They don't want us to see what they put in their potions!*

Jennie, Sam and Beth noticed that sometimes an animal disappeared. The snake was the first to go. Then the lizard.

I know what's happening! They're putting those poor animals in the pot. They're making a witches' brew!

One afternoon a small tattered kitten appeared. That day the witches spent a lot of time mixing a weird potion on the stove. They fed it to the kitten and tittered about whether it was fat enough.

Sam was suspicious. *Fat enough! That doesn't sound good.* She nudged Jennie's leg. *Ask them where all these animals go.*

Jennie took a deep breath and asked politely, "Where did the snake go? And the green lizard?"

"That nice little green lizard?" High Heels fluttered her lashes. "You might say he moved on." She looked at her sisters and giggled.

I know where he went! They've eaten him!

Jennie's stomach heaved.

The witches went into the kitchen to mix the kitten's potion. Jennie leaned over to Beth. "Sam thinks they're eating those animals," she whispered.

Beth's stomach rolled. "I hope your mom comes soon."

At suppertime the telephone rang. It was Jennie's mother saying she had to stay late at the drugstore. Pumpkin poked her head out of the kitchen. "Don't worry. You'll eat supper with us."

"Dinner's in the oven." Spider Lady flashed her pointy teeth. "It's delicious."

"W-w-what is it?" Jennie asked.

"Our secret recipe." Pumpkin clasped her plump hands together. "We love it."

Sam's stomach slammed into her throat. *They've cooked that green lizard! One day he's living his life. The next day he's whammed by a spell and — Presto! He's dinner.*

"Stop it, Sam." Jennie clapped her hands over her mouth. "I'll throw up if you say any more."

It's not my fault if you throw up. I'm not the weird one here.

"I feel awful." Beads of sweat gathered on Beth's forehead. "We can't eat here."

"I'm sick!" Jennie shouted. "I have to go home."

"You can't go home," Pumpkin ordered, her face hard. "Dinner is ready."

"Sam doesn't have to eat, of course," sang High Heels.

Sam breathed a huge sigh of relief. *Sometimes, I love being a dog.*

Jennie shot Sam a terrible look. Beth turned a dull shade of green.

The girls picked at the pot pie the witches dished onto their plates. Jennie nibbled a carrot and Beth chewed at a bit of crust. Little pieces of white meat floated in the gravy. Jennie and Beth looked at the meat in horror.

With her paws over her nose, Sam cowered in a corner of the kitchen. *My appetite is ruined forever.*

At last they heard a knock. High Heels tottered to the door.

"Sorry I'm late!" panted Mrs. Levinsky. "The

whole town came to the drugstore right at closing time."

"No problem," trilled Pumpkin. "We made plenty of food." Her face fell. "Only, the girls didn't seem to like it."

"It was delicious," said Jennie quickly. "But we had a big lunch."

Beth nodded. "A huge lunch! We're still full."

"Well, it was very nice of you to give them dinner," said Jennie's mother. "I hope they weren't any trouble."

"No trouble at all," smiled Spider Lady. "They can stay for dinner any time. We have lots more secret recipes." She looked at her sisters. "Don't we, girls?"

"We certainly do," they sang happily.

10. The Stranger

HE ZAPPED ME! I'M TOAST!

On Friday night, Beth unpacked her sleepover bag and pulled out a cookie tin. "I made cupcakes." She grinned at Sam. "And oatmeal cookies with jelly beans in them."

Sam's head whipped up. *Great! Get some hot salsa for the cupcakes and life will be perfect.*

"I don't have hot salsa, Sam," said Jennie.

Beth rolled her eyes. "Yuck! She wants hot salsa on this stuff?"

At least I don't eat lizards.

Jennie opened the tin and put it beside the pop and chips. "This looks a lot better than the stuff they eat next door."

"Ugh." Beth screwed up her face. "I can't stop

thinking about that poor lizard."

Not only the lizard. How many other animals are missing?

Jennie looked surprised. "How many animals have disappeared over there, Beth?"

Beth counted on her fingers. "That ugly snake. That hideous iguana."

"And the green lizard that went into the pie," added Jennie.

What about that awful-looking parrot?

"Remember that parrot in the sunroom, Beth?" Jennie unrolled the sleeping bag and laid it out on the floor.

"Yeah." Beth nibbled a cookie. "He's gone."

"That's four animals in a week."

Those witches must be chopping the poor little guys up! Mixing them into potions ... Boiling them in stews ... They probably make pickles out of their little toes.

"Stop, Sam!" cried Jennie.

"What's Sam saying?" asked Beth.

Jennie gagged. "She's talking about the witches making pickles out of their toes."

Let's call the police. I bet those crummy witches eat dogs.

"Ugh ... Sam, don't talk about it anymore." Jennie climbed on a chair to get pillows from the closet shelf.

Suddenly Sam's ears pricked up. *Hey! The witches have a visitor!* Poking her head under the curtains, she looked out.

Jennie and Beth pulled back the curtain. On the street below, a black van was parking in front of the neighbors' house.

A tall, thin man dressed in coveralls stepped out and looked up and down the street. As he pulled off heavy leather gloves, he glanced up at their window. Jennie and Beth gasped. He had suspicious eyes, a pointed beard and a black mustache. His face was angry.

Yikes! Another witch! Sam dove under the pillows.

"Get down!" Beth pulled Jennie to the floor beside the bed.

"Sam thinks he's a witch." Jennie grabbed Beth's arm.

He's come for that meeting! Remember the witch book? When they meet to make plans?

Jennie gulped. "Sam says he's come for the witches' meeting."

They listened as footsteps went up the walk and a loud knock sounded on the door.

"Hello, Harold." It was Spider Lady's raspy voice. Then the door shut and there was silence.

Sam went back to the window to watch. For a long time they waited. At last the door opened.

"Tell us what you see, Sam," urged Jennie.

They heard the sisters cooing gushy good-byes.

He's got a cage ... He's taking one of the animals. Sam watched the man walk toward his van. When he opened the rear door, he suddenly turned and glared up at Jennie's window.

Sam felt an odd feeling slither through her

body. *Yikes! He's staring at me! I can't move.*

"Beth! He's staring at Sam!"

"He won't care about Sam. Witches want people, not dogs."

His eyes are going right through me!

"It's okay, Sam," said Jennie. "Beth's right. I never heard of a witch with a dog. They like cats."

He's staring at me so hard I feel weird.

At last the stranger turned away and put the cage in the back of the van. As he opened the driver's door, he gave Sam one last look.

Sam felt it with the force of electricity. *He got me!* She turned away from the window. *That guy zapped me! I'm toast.*

"What do you mean he zapped you?" asked Jennie.

He put a hex on me! Sam groaned and sank onto the bed.

Jennie was puzzled. "How do you know?"

When he looked at me, I felt the spell go right through me. Sam laid her head on the pillow and moaned. *This is bad ... I'm going to change ... I'm*

going to end up in one of those cages ... *If the witches
don't eat me, he'll take me away* ... *I'm doomed.*

Jennie gasped in horror. "Oh no!"

"What is it?" Beth tugged at Jennie's arm.
"Tell me, Jennie!"

"He put a spell on Sam. She felt the hex go
right through her."

Sam sighed. *You just watch. I'm going to turn
into something really disgusting* ...

Like a frog.

11. Witches Making Money?

Sam ate fourteen cupcakes without stopping.

"You'll throw up, Sam," warned Jennie.

I'm going to disappear. I have to eat while I can.

Sam gobbled the last cupcake. *I feel a funny tingling in my paws.* She peered at her toes. *Maybe I'm growing webbed feet. Do I look green? Am I a frog yet?*

"You look fine, Sam," promised Jennie. "You look the same."

I don't feel the same. It's starting in my stomach. I've got a heavy lump there. Sam groaned. *I bet that's where you start to change ... in the middle.*

"Does she look green to you, Beth?"

Beth shook her head. "Nope."

"She has a funny feeling in her feet and a big lump in her stomach."

Beth chewed on a fingernail. "But don't you have to drink a potion to get hexed?"

Relief spread across Jennie's face. "Sure you do." She leaned over and stroked Sam. "Don't worry, Sam. You have to drink a potion for a spell to work."

Forget the potion. I'm no ordinary dog. I know when I've been hexed. Sam moaned loudly. *I'm finished.*

"Sam's sure she's under a spell." Jennie's brown eyes clouded.

Sam belched. *I feel terrible. I think you get sick when you change.*

They looked down at the empty street. Over the rooftops, dark clouds scudded across an orange moon.

"One night we'll see them flying past on their broomsticks," Beth muttered.

In the morning Sam looked at her paws. *No webs yet. I guess a spell takes time to work.*

"Maybe they'd take the spell off if we ask them," said Jennie hopefully. "They seem to like us."

Don't let all that smiling fool you. Witches hate everybody.

At that moment, Jennie glanced out the window. "Hey! There goes another animal!"

Beth and Sam rushed to see. Down the walk scurried the three sisters with a covered cage.

I'm going to follow them. Sam hopped off the bed. *Maybe they're going to a witch club or something. Maybe I can find a way to get this spell off me.*

"Sam wants to follow them!" cried Jennie.

"Good idea, Sam." Beth jumped into jeans and a sweatshirt. "Come on, Jennie."

Jennie, Beth and Sam got to the sidewalk just as the witches rounded the corner.

"After them!" Beth sprinted down the walk. Sam dashed in front and Jennie followed, her long brown hair flying in the wind.

When they got to the corner, they saw the sisters turn at the end of the next block.

They're going to Main Street! Racing ahead, Sam disappeared around the corner.

On Main Street, Sam mingled with the Saturday morning shoppers. When Jennie and Beth caught up, Sam jerked her head toward a store. *They're going in there.*

Flattening themselves against the storefronts, they watched the three sisters sail into the pet store. Through the store window, they saw Pumpkin put the cage on the counter. They smiled and nodded at the owner as if they were best friends.

All this smiling is a trick so nobody will guess they're witches.

"Yeah," muttered Jennie. "Nobody's that nice."

They watched the three sisters take the cover off the cage. Jennie, Beth and Sam craned their necks to see what was inside.

"I've never seen those kittens!" exclaimed Jennie.

"Where did they come from?" wondered Beth.

They watched High Heels hold out her hand while the owner counted money into it.

"He's paying for the kittens!" whispered Jennie.

Sam drew in a sharp breath. *Uh-oh. I know what they're doing ... They're turning people into pets! Then they can sell them!*

Sam stared at Jennie. *Those witches are making money from their spells ... Hey! Wait a minute! Maybe I won't have to be a frog. Nobody buys frogs.*

Then Sam groaned. *Oh no! Maybe I'll be a cat!*

12. Sam Needs Help

Each morning Sam woke up worried. She fretted as she looked in the mirror to see if she was changing.

In Jennie's room on Sunday afternoon, Sam suddenly got angry. *This is an emergency, and you're not helping me.*

"Of course we're helping!" Jennie looked hurt.

Phooey. Those witches are changing me so they can sell me to the pet store. Sam climbed up on Jennie's bed and glared. *I'm doomed, and you're useless.*

"We are not!" Jennie turned to Beth. "Sam says we're useless!"

"We'll help you, Sam," promised Beth. "We

just don't know what to do yet."

Sam's bad mood was getting worse. *So where's my snack? I don't have much time left, and you won't even get me food.* She stared at the wall.

Jennie spread her hands helplessly. "Now Sam's getting mad because I didn't give her a snack."

Sam felt a wave of sadness well up inside her. *Nobody cares about me.*

"Okay. I'll find something." Soon Jennie was back with a bag of peanuts. She dumped them on the bed.

Sam nibbled a peanut and spat. *Blagh!* She slumped down on top of the peanuts. *I only like salty peanuts. And you know it.*

Sam closed her eyes in sorrow. *There you sit while I suffer.*

Jennie put her arm around Sam. "We do care, Sam," she said with great gentleness.

Beth knelt down beside Jennie. "We love you, Sam."

Sam sniffed.

Jennie hugged her tightly. "Please don't be

mad, Sam. We'll find out how to stop the spell."

"We'll need their book of potions to do that," said Beth.

"How will we get it?" Jennie lifted her worried face from Sam's fur.

"We'll just have to look in their house."

"What?"

"There's no other way. We have to get that book." Two bright red spots appeared on Beth's cheeks.

"Maybe the book won't help," said Jennie hopefully.

"If the book tells how to cast a spell, then it will tell how to take one off." Beth clenched her jaw and folded her arms. "We'll find the book. We'll take the spell off, and Sam will be fine."

You'd better work fast. My whole body is tingling now.

"Are you sure we need that book?" Jennie asked.

Sam glared. *I'm under a big spell here. I could use a little help if you don't mind.*

Beth paced back and forth. "Here's what we

need to do." She chewed on a fingernail. "Tomorrow, ask the witches to go for a walk with you."

"And then?"

"I'll stay at the house and look for their book," answered Beth grimly.

Jennie twirled a piece of her hair nervously. "You shouldn't go poking around in a witch's house, Beth. It's dangerous."

Sam shot Jennie a nasty look. *I'll tell you what's dangerous! It's dangerous to turn into a cat or a frog or some other crummy thing. It's dangerous to get cooked up for dinner or sold to a pet store. That's what's dangerous!*

Jennie chewed her lip. "I-I don't know."

Beth's not a wimp like some people I could mention.

Sam sidled over to Beth and glared at Jennie. *Beth is a lovely kid, isn't she?*

Jennie sighed.

13. What Beth Found

When the three friends knocked on the neighbors' door the next day after school, they had a plan.

"We can't back out now," Beth said through clenched teeth. "Sam needs us."

You bet I do.

The door opened. "Hello, dear ones," oozed Pumpkin plumply.

Spider Lady leaned down and smiled thinly at Sam. "You are our very favorite visitor these days."

Tell me something I don't already know.

Just then Rupert peeked around the corner and saw his owner smiling at Sam. "Eeeow!" he shrieked.

Phew! You stink worse than usual today.

"Eeeeow!" screeched Rupert. His torn ear wobbled with rage.

Shut up. Or I'll chomp off your other ear.
"Grrrrr."

Rupert stuck his chewed tail in the air and disappeared. When he was gone, High Heels said cozily, "He gets jealous, poor baby."

Anybody that ugly should get jealous.

When they were all sitting in the living room, Jennie smiled brightly. "Would you like to take Sam for a walk today?"

High Heels tittered. "What a good idea. We could get ice cream."

The three sisters ran for their coats. "I love ice cream," cooed Pumpkin. "I'm going to have a banana split."

Beth waited until they had their coats on. "I hope you don't mind if I wait here," she sighed. "I'm feeling too tired to walk."

Spider Lady turned to the other witches. "We can't leave her here ... alone."

Jennie grinned cheerfully. "Beth stays by

herself all the time!" She turned to Beth before the witches could say anything. "What'll we bring you, Beth?"

"A strawberry sundae! Ple-e-e-ase," cried Beth eagerly.

The sisters looked doubtful.

"We-l-l-l," said Spider Lady slowly.

Beth tried to look exhausted.

"You poor thing," fluttered High Heels. "Beth, we'll be back in ten minutes. Don't worry. We'll bring you a nice treat."

And they were gone.

In the sudden silence, all the tiny eyes in cages turned to Beth. For a moment she listened to the animals' small, watchful movements. Then she headed for the kitchen. She had to find the witches' book. Sam was counting on her.

Beth felt as if she couldn't breathe. Carefully she looked in every kitchen drawer and cupboard. Nothing.

Her nose twitched when she walked by the smelly brown brew on the stove. She looked through all the cookbooks on the shelf. The book of spells and potions should be there — but it wasn't.

Beth looked in the sunroom, the living room and the dining room. No book.

In the back hall there was a door into the garage. Beth crept toward it. She twisted the door handle and opened it — just a crack.

Beth peered in and looked around the garage. Garden tools, a lawn mower, garbage cans, boxes, empty cages.

Suddenly, from somewhere in the garage came mewling noises, like small creatures in pain. Beth's hand gripped the doorknob as she listened. Very slowly she opened the door wider.

In the corner under a heat lamp stood a cage lined with straw. Staring sadly at her through the wire were skinny yellow puppies. Beth walked over and looked at them closely. They were dazed and listless.

The witches had these puppies under a spell! Shocked, Beth retraced her steps to the living room. The moment she sat down, Sam and Jennie and the witches came in with ice cream.

Eating it seemed to take forever. Sam gobbled hers from a bowl. Then she fidgeted while she watched the witches chatter and slurp.

I've got to find out if Beth got the book.

When Jennie's mother came, the three friends thanked the sisters and shot out the door. Mrs. Levinsky watched them in amazement.

"Did you get the book?" Jennie demanded as soon as they got to her room.

Beth shook her head. "I couldn't find it. But I found puppies in the garage!"

Jennie was shocked. "What were they doing?"

"They were just lying in their cage, staring.

They weren't normal, Jennie. They looked sick."

Don't expect anything normal in there. Those witches are weird.

Jennie was puzzled. "I've never heard of witches wanting dogs."

Sam started to pace. *They're going to sell them to the pet store!* Her mind whirred. *Maybe it's not just people they change ... Maybe they collect ugly things like toads and frogs and bald guinea pigs ... If they don't eat them, they change them into puppies and kittens so they can sell them!*

"Sam thinks they change ugly animals into puppies or kittens so they can sell them."

Suddenly Sam had a new and terrible thought. *You don't suppose they'll change me back to a puppy! I'd have to go through all that training ... People would whack me with newspapers ... Kids would pick me up and squish me ...* She sat down with a thud. *I couldn't take it.*

Jennie looked at Sam with sympathy. She wished they had never set eyes on those neighbors.

14. Jennie Keeps Watch

Every night before she went to sleep, Jennie watched the neighbors from her bedroom window. And almost every night the angry stranger took cages in or brought cages out. Sometimes he scowled up at Jennie's window.

Whenever the stranger looked at her, Jennie panicked. "I can't watch anymore," she told Beth after a week. "I'll be hexed like Sam."

Beth had an idea. "We need a periscope. Then we can watch without being seen."

"Noel used to have one." Jennie thought for a moment. "I wonder where it is?"

After school, Jennie and Beth rooted around in Noel's closet until they found his periscope.

They took it to Jennie's room and hooked it over the windowsill. They could see outside perfectly.

With the curtains closed and the periscope sticking up over the window ledge, Jennie felt safer. Yet every time the mysterious stranger glared up at the window, her heart stopped.

"You look tired, Jennie," said her mother at breakfast one day. "Are you sleeping all right?"

Jennie squirmed as everyone turned to look at her. "I'm fine," she mumbled.

"You'll have to go to bed a half hour earlier," said her mom firmly. "That's all there is to it."

Noel chuckled merrily through his toast.

On Saturday morning, Jennie, Beth and Sam followed the witches up Main Street. They watched as the pet-shop owner took the cage and paid for his prize.

After the witches left, Jennie, Beth and Sam

went into the pet store. The owner looked at them over his spectacles. He had white hair and a round jolly face. "I bet you kids would like a goldfish." He grinned at Sam. "How about some dog food?"

Ugh. Don't mention the stuff.

"We're just looking, thank you." Jennie tried to sound polite.

"We love to look at puppies," Beth said innocently.

The owner's blue eyes crinkled cheerfully. "You do? Then follow me." He led them to the back of the store and showed them a cage of puppies.

Beth gasped.

"Aren't they cute?" The owner chuckled. "But you can't buy them. They're already sold."

Just then the shop bell rang. "Be right back." The owner turned and went to the front of the store.

Beth's eyes were glued to the cage. "Those are the puppies I saw in the witches' garage! But they look normal now."

Sam went over to the cage and sniffed. *Say, you guys, do you remember being toads or frogs before you were puppies?*

The puppies just looked at her with soft brown eyes.

Think hard. Do you remember hopping around in the woods?

The puppies wiggled their stubby tails.

"What's Sam doing?" whispered Beth.

"She's trying to find out if they remember being toads or frogs. But they don't understand."

On the way out, Jennie, Beth and Sam stopped to look at the fish. When the shop bell rang and the door opened, their knees turned to jelly.

It was the stranger!

"D-d-don't let him see us!" whispered Jennie.

Beth flattened herself against an aquarium.

"Quick!" Jennie whipped off her jacket. "We have to hide Sam." She threw the jacket over Sam's head.

Jennie and Beth huddled in front of Sam.

The stranger's black eyes glittered. He had a hard line for a mouth and an angry twitch in his jaw. He looked around at the shelves and cages. Then he looked straight at Jennie and Beth!

15. A Dangerous Search

If he stared at you, he cast a spell on you. You're finished — just like me. Sam crawled up on Jennie's bed and snuffled in an empty chip bag.

Jennie felt a shiver of fear race through her. "Sam thinks he put a spell on us, Beth."

"That's what I think, too." Beth stared out the window. "We've got to get these spells off." She gritted her teeth.

Suddenly Beth leaned forward. "Wait a minute! There they go with another cage!"

Jennie and Sam looked out. The witches scuttled down the walk and headed toward Main Street.

Hey! Sam nudged Jennie with her nose. *They*

didn't lock the door!

Jennie looked surprised. "Why do you care?"

I care a lot. I'm going to get the spell book! Come on.

"They didn't lock the door. Is that what Sam's talking about?" Beth turned from the window.

Jennie rolled her eyes. "Sam wants to go in there and find the book."

Sam hopped off the bed. *This is a matter of life and death.* She scratched on the bedroom door. *Did I ever tell you how much I hate wimps?*

Beth opened the door for Sam. "I'm going with you, Sam. We need that book."

Jennie gasped. "We can't just go into people's houses!" But Beth and Sam were already downstairs.

Reluctantly Jennie followed.

When they got to the neighbors' front door, Beth reached for the handle and turned. The door opened and the empty hallway yawned before them.

Follow me. Sam pushed through the door. Before Jennie and Beth could stop her, Sam bounded up the stairs.

"We've got no choice, Jennie." Beth clenched her fists. "We have to go in. We have to break the spells."

"I know." Jennie gulped.

Together they stepped into the witches' house.

From the living room came a loud yowl. Rupert glared at them with his one hateful eye. Then he streaked past them out the front door.

They listened for a moment. The house felt strangely alive. All around them were tiny sounds — faint squeaks and whines and whimpers.

Up the stairs they went, into the dimness of the upper hallway. Sam sniffed her way to the far end and pawed at a closed door.

When Beth opened the door, they saw a storeroom filled with boxes and cages. From one cage some tiny puppies looked at them. Listless and sad, the puppies didn't move.

Hi, guys. Sam sidled up to the puppies in a friendly way. *Have you seen those witches with a recipe book?*

The puppies just stared with dull eyes.

Sam snuffled around the cages. *Are you sure you haven't seen those witches holding a book?* The puppies looked at her dazedly.

"What have they done to these poor puppies?" Jennie cried.

"They look really sick," whispered Beth.

So would you if you were supposed to be a frog or a guinea pig. Let me tell you, these spells make a person feel terrible. I should know. Did I mention that my knees hurt now?

A prickly feeling was spreading up the back of Jennie's neck. "Don't waste any time! It's spooky in here."

"Yeah." Beth looked around at boxes, cages and bits of furniture. "I don't see anything that looks like a book."

Sam was poking the puppies with her wet nose. *Do you remember being toads or frogs before you were puppies?*

"Sam! We have to hurry!" hissed Jennie. "Come on!"

Jennie, Sam and Beth rushed back to the

hallway, slamming the door behind them.

"Quick!" Beth yanked Jennie's arm. "I'll look in the first room. You look in the next one."

Beth opened a door, went in and looked frantically. Nothing.

Jennie went into the next room and searched. Her heart thudded in her ears. No book.

Then Beth flung open the door of the third room. They both ran in and looked around.

"The book's not here," whispered Jennie, panicking. "We've got to go! Come on, Sam!"

They ran to the end of the hall and headed for the stairway.

On the top step, they stopped dead in their tracks, their eyes glued to the front door.

The handle was turning!

In horror they watched the door open slowly. A man walked in. As he pulled off his gloves, finger by finger, he looked around the front hall.

It was the mysterious stranger.

16. Trapped!

YIKES! HERE COMES ANOTHER SPELL.

Hugging the walls, they slunk back down the hallway. Very carefully, Beth turned the knob on the storeroom door.

It squeaked!

They froze. They waited for the stranger to swoop down on them.

When nothing happened, they crept into the storeroom and closed the door quietly. Beth pointed to a pile of boxes in a corner. Without a word they crawled behind them.

They held their breath as heavy boots thudded up the stairs and down the hallway.

Closer and closer ...

Squeeeeak. The door opened.

The three friends crouched in terror. Sam was seeing spots in front of her eyes, and her whole body tingled. *Yikes! I'm changing right now!*

The stranger walked over to the puppies' cage. Huddling together, the puppies shrank back. Their little bodies quivered.

"You're not ready yet," he said in a deep growly voice. "They need to fatten you up."

He looked at the puppies for a long time and then turned to go.

The stranger's boots thudded down the stairs and clicked through the front hall. The front door opened and closed. Then there was silence.

Outside they heard the van door slam. The engine started and the van pulled away. The three friends listened until the sound of the motor disappeared.

"He's gone," whispered Jennie at last.

"Let's get out of here," hissed Beth. "The witches will be back any minute!" She ran to the door.

They'll slap another spell on us.

"Hurry!" Jennie climbed out from behind the boxes.

Just as they were starting down the stairs, they heard voices coming up the walk.

They stopped.

Spider Lady's raspy voice wafted through the door. "I like Mr. Prim at the pet shop so much."

The front door swung open and Rupert streaked in. Chattering happily, the witches stepped into the hall.

Without a sound, Jennie, Beth and Sam sneaked back to the storeroom. They slipped through the door and hid behind the boxes again. Muffled voices moved toward the kitchen. The sound of rattling dishes drifted upstairs.

"What'll we do?" whispered Jennie, fighting a terrible panic.

Beth's mouth was dry. "They'll get us now," she whispered. "We don't have a chance."

I'll think of something. You're lucky I'm such a smart detective.

Jennie looked at Sam in disbelief. "You're the one who got us into this, so you are definitely not smart."

"Yeah, Sam," added Beth in an angry whisper. "This was your idea. Remember?"

Sam shrugged. *So we've got a little problem.*

"A little problem? You crazy dog!" Jennie was turning bright red. "I don't call getting boiled in a witches' brew a little problem!"

Phooey. Stop insulting me or I won't get us out of here.

"Sam," hissed Jennie through clenched teeth. "There is no way out of here. And there are three witches downstairs!"

There's always a way out. Any smart detective knows that.

Beth was looking at the open window. "Maybe we could go out the window."

I told you. There's always a way.

Jennie was doubtful. "It looks high."

Beth tiptoed over to the window and leaned out. "There's a drainpipe that goes to the shed roof. We can climb down."

Perfect. You can come back and get me later. That is, if you recognize me. I might be a gerbil by then ... or a turtle ... or a cat.

Jennie's eyes filled with sudden tears. "I don't want to leave you, Sam."

This is no time to get wimpy. Here's what you do. Climb down, and come back to visit the witches. Leave the front door open a crack. Keep them busy so I can sneak out.

Jennie repeated the plan to Beth. "Brilliant!" said Beth admiringly. "You sure are a smart dog, Sam."

Glad you noticed.

Giving Sam one last hug, Beth disappeared out the window.

Jennie put her leg over the sill. "Stay behind the boxes until you hear us talking, Sam."

Don't start giving me orders about my own brilliant plan.

Hurry! I might change any minute!

17. Lost!

Silently Beth and Jennie climbed down the drainpipe onto the shed roof. The sound of clinking dishes wafted out the window.

Beth pointed. "Let's jump down to that bench."

Jennie swung her legs over the side of the shed. Beth did the same. They landed on the bench with a dull thud. Without a word, they scrambled over the fence into Jennie's back yard.

In minutes the two girls were back, knocking on the neighbors' front door.

"Sisters!" sang High Heels when she opened it, "It's Jennie and Beth come to visit."

Pumpkin poked her head out. "I love surprise visitors!"

Beth sniffed the air and started walking toward the kitchen. "Something smells good!" she said in a loud voice.

Jennie sniffed hard. "What are you making?" she shouted up the stairs. "You sure are good cooks!"

While the witches watched Beth sniff her way over to the kitchen, Jennie left the front door ajar for Sam.

"Sure smells yummy!" screamed Beth. High Heels jumped.

"Somebody's cooking something delicious!" hollered Jennie, heading for the kitchen.

Bewildered, the witches followed the girls. "Would you like to sit down?" asked Spider Lady.

"I'd rather see what you're cooking!" shouted Jennie.

"We love to cook!" yelled Beth. "Don't we, Jennie?"

High Heels put her hands over her ears. Her

eyelashes fluttered. "Why are you two yelling?"

Jennie gulped. "We're not yelling, are we?"

Pumpkin folded her plump arms and looked at them strangely. "You are screaming at the top of your lungs."

The witches exchanged glances. "Why are you yelling?" repeated High Heels, her false eyelashes very still.

"Ear infections!" screamed Beth suddenly. "We can't hear anything."

"Right!" shouted Jennie. "We have colds! Our ears are plugged." She continued sniffing her way through the kitchen door.

Spider Lady squinted at them. "When people have colds they can't smell food."

Jennie and Beth looked at each other.

"We must be getting better then!" cried Jennie.

"Yeah," sang Beth cheerfully. "We can smell your cooking, so we must be getting better."

The three sisters looked at one another oddly. "It's just ordinary spaghetti sauce," said Pumpkin quietly.

"We love it!" smiled Jennie.

"Love it!" repeated Beth.

"Sit down then," said Spider Lady firmly. "We'll give you some."

"Yum!" sang Jennie. "That's really nice of you."

"Wow!" chimed in Beth. "How did you know we were hungry?"

"We guessed," said Pumpkin dryly. "Sit down."

Jennie and Beth smiled brightly. Spider Lady gave them some spaghetti and sauce. They ate it as slowly as they could. Then they thanked the sisters loudly and backed out of the kitchen.

The three sisters watched them in silence, an odd look on their faces.

"Whew!" gasped Jennie, sinking onto a deck chair in her back yard. "Where's Sam?"

Beth looked around the yard.

"Sam!" shouted Jennie getting up off the chair. "Sam!"

Sam didn't answer. "Sam! Sam! Where are you?" They poked behind bushes. "Sam! Come out. Don't play games!"

But there was no sign of Sam. Jennie's heart sank.

All afternoon they looked. They searched Jennie's house from top to bottom. They looked in the neighbors' yards. They checked Beth's house. They went to the pet store. They even searched Sam's house when Joan and Bob were out.

Hopelessness washed over them like a wave. Sam was gone.

"Sam must have changed," said Jennie in a small voice.

"Maybe she turned into something so tiny she couldn't get down the stairs." Beth's voice faltered.

"I wonder what poor Sam has become." Jennie's eyes filled with tears.

"Caw! Caw!" They looked up to see the crow

perched on the roof. Its bright eyes gleamed. "Caw!"

A sudden shiver crawled up Jennie's back. "It seems to be telling us something."

"Probably that Sam is gone forever." Beth put her chin in her hands. Tears ran down her cheeks.

Jennie buried her face in her arms. "What are we going to do?"

Beth had no answer.

18. All Alone

In the storeroom Sam waited and waited until she heard Jennie and Beth. Then she wriggled out from behind the cartons. *I'm out of here!*

Sam squeezed through the crack in the door and padded along the hall. Creeping down the stairs, she chuckled at Jennie and Beth yelling about the wonderful spaghetti sauce.

Sam headed for the front door. Something didn't look right. *Wait a minute!* Her heart sank. *Somebody's shut the door!*

Sam tried to twist the doorknob with her teeth but it wouldn't turn. *Uh-oh. This is bad. Very bad.*

Sam heard the girls saying goodbye loudly. In

a flash she darted up the stairs and squeezed in behind the boxes.

She heard the front door close with a thud. Jennie and Beth were gone.

Terrible loneliness washed over Sam. *I'll never see Jennie and Beth again ... I'll turn into a lizard and those witches will toss me into their stinking brew ... I'm finished.* Sam sniffled quietly.

Muffled sounds surrounded Sam's prison — closing doors, rattling dishes, television, music. For hours Sam sat there, longing for her friends.

Then, without warning, the door opened. "Now, baby. Tell mama what bothers you about this room," crooned Pumpkin.

"Eeow!"

Sam's heart sank. *All right, baby. Get ready for one good chomp.*

"He's been pacing back and forth up here all afternoon," grunted Spider Lady. "Something's the matter."

Sam braced herself. *This is it! When I finish with baby, I'll bite everybody ... I'll capture the witches ... I'll be a hero ... Nobody knows they've*

got witches living in Woodford ... I'll get my picture
in the newspaper ... I'll get a reward and I'll be rich.
Rich is good.

As Sam waited for the repulsive Rupert, a tiny growl rumbled deep in her throat.

"Eow!" screamed Rupert.

"You don't suppose there's a mouse behind those boxes?" fluttered High Heels.

"Eeeow!" howled Rupert.

Just as Sam was about to leap, the doorbell rang.

"You'll have to show us the mouse later," said High Heels.

"Eeeeoow!" screeched Rupert.

"Don't be silly, Rupert," croaked Spider Lady. "Don't you want to see who's at the door? We'll get the mouse later."

They all went downstairs.

And Sam was alone again.

19. Sam Has a Bad Idea

THESE WITCHES ARE GETTING ON MY NERVES.

Sam got hungry. She also got thirsty and depressed. *I'd be a hero if I didn't have that spell on me. I'm brave enough. I'm smart enough. But just when I take my first chomp, I'll go up in a puff of smoke ... I'll turn into a mouse and that disgusting cat will eat me.*

I can't bite anybody when I'm going to change.

The more she thought about it, the crabbier Sam got. *As soon as that front door opens, I'm out of here. Watch out, witches! I'm hungry and I'm mad.*

"Maybe we should go to the witches' house one more time," suggested Beth.

"Yeah. We can look for a little animal trying to get out the door."

"Let's do it," said Beth.

When they got to the witches' door, Beth knocked. "We've come to visit again," she said loudly when the door opened.

High Heels looked puzzled. "Another visit!"

"I hope we're not too much trouble!" shouted Jennie, smiling widely.

Spider Lady stuck her head around the doorway. "Jennie and Beth? Again?"

Pumpkin appeared. She raised her eyebrows in surprise.

Jennie opened her mouth to say something when they heard a thundering sound upstairs. Thump! Thump! Thump! Sam clambered down the stairs. Crashing into the witches, she sent Pumpkin sprawling against the wall. High Heels wavered on her ridiculous shoes.

"Sam!" shouted Jennie.

Sam shot out the front door. *Let's get out of*

here. I'm hungry!

"What on earth?" cried Spider Lady.

"I guess we'll be going!" sang out Beth with a toothy smile.

Jennie waved. "Thank you for the nice visit! Bye!"

"Just a minute!" shouted High Heels. "What is going on here?"

"What's Sam doing in our house?" demanded Spider Lady.

But Sam, Jennie and Beth were gone. Sam streaked across Jennie's yard — with the girls behind her.

No one was home at Jennie's house. There was a note on the kitchen table saying that Noel would be back in a half an hour.

Before long, the witches were banging on Jennie's front door.

"Lock it," whispered Beth. Jennie did.

Bang! Bang!

Jennie and Beth raced around the house locking all the doors and windows.

Hey! Where's the food? I need pop ... gallons of pop. Wow! Was I brave! Anyone else would have cracked under the pressure — but not me.

Jennie pulled the curtains shut. "I don't want those witches looking in."

Forget them. I want pretzels with grape jelly and ketchup. And pancakes. And sardines with hot salsa. I'm starving here, in case anybody cares!

Jennie grabbed a bottle of pop and a bag of cookies, and they rushed up to her room.

Knocking and banging echoed through the house.

Nervously, Beth nibbled the edge of a cookie. "I bet those witches are going to be even more dangerous now."

Jennie nodded, her brown eyes wide. "They're probably going to get in here with their magic."

Sam slurped at the pop and crunched cookies. *I'm getting fed up with these witches. What happened to the pretzels with grape jelly and ketchup?*

Suddenly the banging stopped. Muffled voices came through the door.

Jennie lifted a corner of the curtain. What she saw made her blood run cold. The mysterious stranger was talking to the witches. He kept looking up at Jennie's window.

Jennie ducked. "That man's here! They're talking about us! They must know we've been spying on them!"

Beth hooked the periscope over the windowsill. The stranger was pointing to Jennie's window! "We're in trouble! He's hexing us!"

Dragging the cookie bag with her, Sam crawled under the bed. *I'm not letting that guy zap me twice.*

"I wish my parents would come home," squeaked Jennie.

Even Noel the teenage oaf would be nice to have around right now.

The silence was shattered by the doorbell. Beth looked through the periscope again.

"They're not out there anymore." Her voice was hollow.

The doorbell rang again. Very quietly, Jennie, Beth and Sam crept to the top of the stairs, where they could see the front door.

"Good thing we locked it." Jennie's voice was small.

The letter flap flipped open.

"Jennie, dear." Pumpkin's gushiest voice wafted through the door. "Your mother called and asked if we would baby-sit you. Noel is making an extra delivery for the drugstore, and you'll be alone too long."

The three friends didn't move.

"Jennie," sang High Heels. "Bring Beth and Sam, too. We made a little surprise. It was for tomorrow but we can have it today."

Sam flinched. *Just what I need, another surprise.*

"Your mother doesn't want you to stay alone, dear," rasped Spider Lady sweetly. "She's worried about you. And so are we."

In horror, Jennie, Beth and Sam watched the door handle rattle. They heard muttered conversation behind the door.

"Call your mother," breathed Beth.

"My parents think these witches are wonderful. Nothing will change their minds."

They'll change their minds when we're all toads.

The letter flap was flipping open again. "Jennie dear," crooned Pumpkin through the slit. "Come back to our house. We're supposed to look after you."

A new sound came up the stairs. Now there was rattling at the back door!

"We have a lovely surprise for you," trilled High Heels from the back.

I wish they'd quit talking about surprises.

All the door handles rattled.

These witches are getting on my nerves. How can anybody make me a hamburger with all this going on? I'm hungry. And I'm tired of everybody being scared.

"S-Sam's sick of us being scared," said Jennie.

These witches are making wimps out of us. I hate wimps.

Beth folded her arms firmly. "Sam's right. I'm sick of it, too. I want to do something."

Dump water on them. Then get me some food.

Jennie was startled. "Sam wants us to dump water on them."

A huge grin spread over Beth's tiny face. "Good idea, Sam."

Hurry up then. I need a hamburger with butterscotch sauce.

Beth ran to the bathroom, dumped out the wastebasket and filled it with water.

What are you waiting for? Sam glared at Jennie impatiently. *I want these creeps out of here. I'm hungry.*

Jennie grabbed the wastebaskets from all the bedrooms. She put them in the tub to fill.

Wheedling voices came through the door. "We know you're in there. Please come to our house."

Beth and Jennie carried the wastebaskets to the window in Noel's room. Very quietly they opened the window and leaned out. They were right above the front door – and the three witches. Sam put her paws on the windowsill so she could see.

Just as the witches stepped back from the door, Jennie and Beth let the water go.

The witches screamed as the water poured over their heads.

"This is outrageous!" they screeched, when Jennie and Beth doused them again.

"Eow!" they howled, as the next load of water hit. They sounded exactly like Rupert.

"Turn yourselves into toads!" yelled Jennie as she hoisted the next wastebasket.

"We're not scared of you anymore!" hollered Beth, throwing out another load of water.

"Woof!" barked Sam. "Woof!"

At that moment Jennie's parents arrived.

20. The Truth About the Witches

ONE LITTLE MISTAKE.

Jennie's parents were furious. "Jennie! Beth! Get down here this minute!"

Outraged and dripping, the witches stood in the front hall.

Jennie and Beth slunk downstairs. Sam stayed at the top. *This is going to be boring. There'll be shouting. There'll be lectures.* Sam sighed. *I'm glad I'm a dog.*

Sam went back into Jennie's bedroom, polished off the cookies and drank the rest of the pop. Whiny witch voices, angry parent voices, and small Beth and Jennie voices drifted up the stairs.

When the food was gone, Sam went down to the living room. Jennie and Beth were perched on chairs. The witches were wrapped in bath towels. High Heels had black mascara streaming down her face. Pumpkin had flat hair. Spider Lady looked like a drowned rat.

"What makes you girls so sure our nice neighbors are witches?" Jennie's father was asking.

"The potions they're always boiling on the stove," offered Jennie.

The witches giggled.

"The way the little animals disappear," piped up Beth.

The witches rolled their eyes.

"The trained toads the movers dropped," added Jennie.

The witches snorted.

"The strange man who collects the animals they've put under a spell!" cried Beth.

The witches raised their eyebrows.

"The way they cooked up that poor lizard and tried to make us eat it!" put in Jennie.

The witches tittered behind their hands.

"The storms when the witches started their

magic," said Beth.

The witches cackled.

Sam glared at the witches. *Nice try. Throw everybody off the trail by cackling your witchy heads off.* Sam turned to Jennie. *Tell your parents we've got spells on us.*

Jennie looked doubtful.

It's proof. When we change, they'll know we told the truth.

Jennie looked up at her parents. "That man who comes to their house is a witch, too — and he put spells on us. Sam and Beth and I are all going to change into little animals. Then you'll know we've told the truth."

Mr. and Mrs. Levinsky stared at her, open-mouthed.

Holding their sides, the witches shrieked with laughter.

Sam sniffed. *Listen to them laugh, Jennie. It's proof that they're wicked witches with no hearts.*

Coughing, sputtering and doubled up with laughter, the witches staggered to the door. "We're going home to change our clothes," giggled Pumpkin. "Come over in twenty minutes. We'll explain everything."

She cackled as she went out the door.

Very funny.

In the witches' living room, Jennie, Beth and Sam huddled together. On the big sofa, Jennie's mother and father sat with Beth's parents. The witches were still laughing.

Stop laughing and get started on your lies.

Pumpkin bustled in with tea and lemonade. "We've had a little misunderstanding, that's all." She poured tea. "But there are no hard feelings. Right, sisters?"

"Certainly not," tittered High Heels.

"Forgive and forget," chuckled Spider Lady.

Rupert yowled at the visitors with glittering hatred.

Pumpkin sat down and beamed at everyone. "See all these little animals?" She motioned to cages holding a skinny kitten, a tufty hamster, a blotchy iguana and a straggly rabbit.

Everyone nodded.

"They're not under a spell." She giggled so much her frizzy hair shook.

Spit it out.We're getting bored.

"We're foster parents!" said Spider Lady.

"Foster parents?" Beth looked blank.

The witches nodded happily. "We take in mistreated animals. We fatten them up and nurse them back to health."

"Fatten them up?" Jennie looked stunned.

The witches nodded again.

"Before we can find new homes for them, they have to be healthy." High Heels fluttered her lashes. "That's our job."

"You – you don't eat them?" Jennie squinted narrowly at the witches.

Peals of witchy laughter echoed around the room.

"Certainly not!" Spider Lady took off her glasses and wiped her eyes. "We're helping them, not eating them!"

"But what do you boil in that brew?" Beth chewed on a fingernail.

"That's a tonic for the animals. It's full of herbs and vitamins. We put it down their little throats with eyedroppers. They don't like it much, but it brings them right back to health," said Pumpkin.

"Those little bottles are really vitamins?" asked Jennie.

The witches nodded.

Ask them about the toads.

"What about those toads that escaped on moving day?"

High Heels fluttered her lashes. "Those toads had a terrible life. They were rescued from an experiment."

"We shouldn't have tried to ship them in a crate." Pumpkin shook her head sadly.

Beth watched the witches closely. "So you were going to look after the toads?"

The witches nodded. "Poor little things."

Hmph. Ask them about the stranger.

"What about that strange man who comes to

your house?" asked Jennie.

"Harold?" Pumpkin smiled sweetly. "He has the most heartbreaking job. He's an animal rescuer. He brings them to us."

"But he takes animals away!" cried Beth.

"Away?" Pumpkin looked blank for a moment. "Of course! He takes them to the pet store for us. Some animals are too heavy for us to carry. Mr. Prim at the pet store finds the animals new homes."

"But Mr. Prim gives you money," objected Jennie.

"Certainly." High Heels fluttered her lashes. "Mr. Prim charges the new owners a little fee and gives it to us to help with the rescue work."

"It's very important work," added Pumpkin, pouring more tea. "These animals have been badly treated and they need good homes."

That guy doesn't look like some nice guy who rescues animals.

Jennie took a deep breath. "Why is Harold so angry?"

Spider Lady leaned forward. "He can't stand

seeing animals suffer. Poor Harold gets in such a state."

So why did he stare at me like I'm a criminal or something?

"Why did he stare at Sam all the time?" Jennie asked.

Pumpkin laughed. "Harold says every time he sees a fat dog like Sam, it makes him angry for all the skinny animals who don't get enough to eat."

Sam gasped. *Fat! I've never been fat in my life! I'm beautiful. Look at yourself. Now that's fat.*

All the parents gooed and gushed and said the sisters were so lovely, how could anybody have thought they were witches?

Jennie and Beth glared at Sam.

Okay. Okay. So I made one little mistake.

A few days later, Sam was waiting for Jennie to come after school. She stretched out on the sofa

and thought about all the stories she loved —
witches, giants, fairies, goblins and monsters ...
There's got to be something exciting going on
in Woodford.

"Sam!"

Sam hopped off the sofa and wiggled happily
at Jennie. *About time you got here. I'm bored and I'm
starving.*

"Come on, Sam. Beth and I have something
to show you."

*Is it a mystery? Is it scary? Is it exciting? Does it
need a good detective?*

Jennie smiled. "It's not a mystery, Sam. But
it's great."

Jennie led Sam up to her bedroom. Beth was
sitting on the bed with two cages.

Who are these guys?

"This is Albert." Jennie held up a bald guinea
pig. "He eats lettuce."

Lettuce! Aggh! No wonder he went bald.

Beth held up a bedraggled kitten. "I'm naming
her Rosie." She kissed Rosie's tufty head. The
kitten drew back tiny pink lips and meowed.

"Just think, Sam," said Jennie proudly, "Beth and I are foster parents!"

Sam looked at Rosie's little blue eyes and Albert's bright black ones, and she felt a rush of pity. *Poor little guys. They haven't had much luck.*

All the same ... they better not interfere with our adventures. I have to find a new mystery.

And I have to find it right now.

SPYING ON DRACULA

Sam, Dog Detective, sniffs out adventure!

Ten-year-old Jennie Levinsky has a secret — and only her best friend, Beth, knows about it. Jennie can "hear" what her neighbor's sheepdog, Sam, is thinking! And what Sam is thinking leads the girls into an exciting adventure at the spookiest house in town. Why is the house always dark? Why is a bat always hanging around? And who is that frightening creature living inside? Sam comes to the only logical conclusion — Dracula lives there!

THE GHOST OF CAPTAIN BRIGGS

Sam, Dog Detective, digs up a mystery!

Jennie and Beth are all set to enjoy their summer vacation with Sam. But how could they know that the house Jennie's family has rented was built long ago by a bloodthirsty pirate? Sam convinces Jennie that where there's a pirate, there must be buried treasure ... and a ghost guarding it. What else could explain the spooky housekeeper, the threatening notes and those eerie sounds coming from the attic? Then Sam digs up a hidden tunnel ... but does it lead to treasure or danger?